Once upon a time, an old farmer and his wife grew turnips on their farm.

One of the turnips
looked enormous.

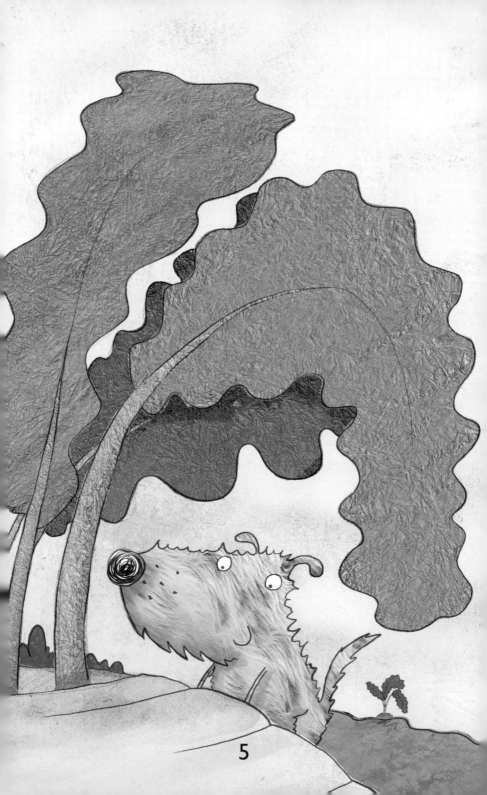

"I'll pull up that enormous turnip now," said the farmer.

"Yes, then we can have turnip soup for supper," agreed his wife.

The farmer gave the enormous turnip a gentle tug.

But the turnip did
not move.

The farmer pulled
and pulled.

Still the turnip did
not move.

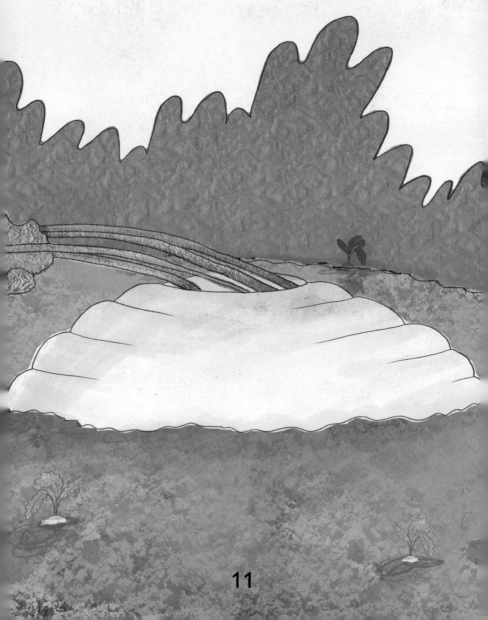

The farmer called to his
wife for help.

The farmer and his wife
pulled and pulled.

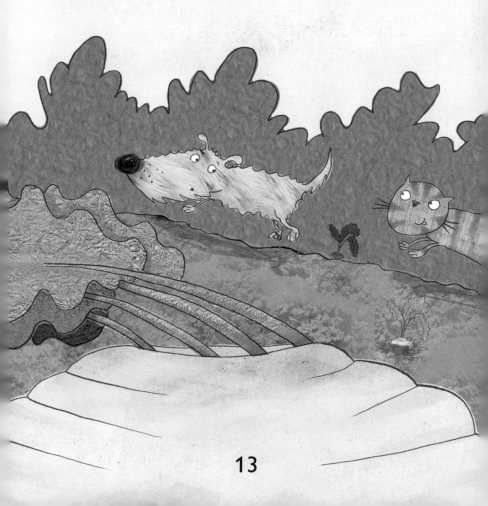

Still the turnip did not move.

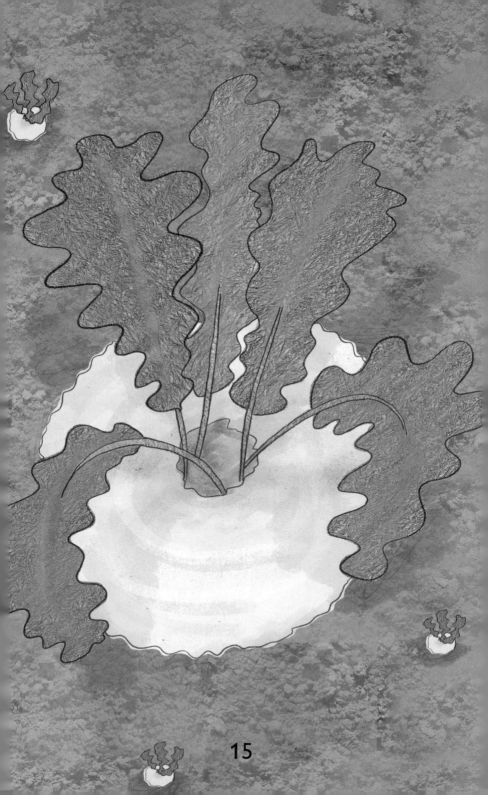

The farmer's wife whistled
to the dog for help.

The farmer, his wife and the dog pulled and pulled.

Still the turnip did
not move.

So the dog barked
to the cat for help.

The farmer, his wife,
the dog and the cat
pulled and pulled.

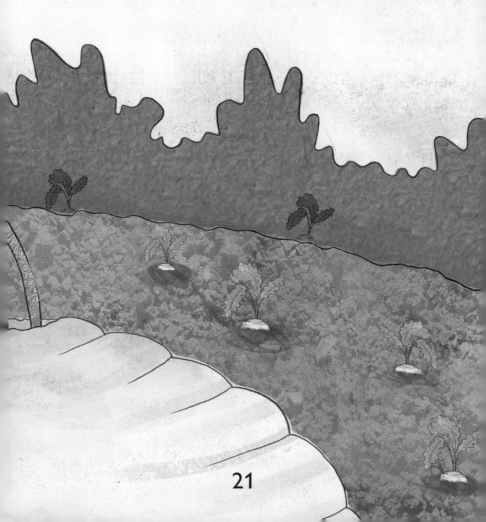

Still the turnip did
not move.

"It's no good. This turnip is stuck!" sighed the farmer.

Then the cat meowed to
a little bird for help.

The farmer, his wife, the dog, the cat and the little bird pulled and pulled and pulled.

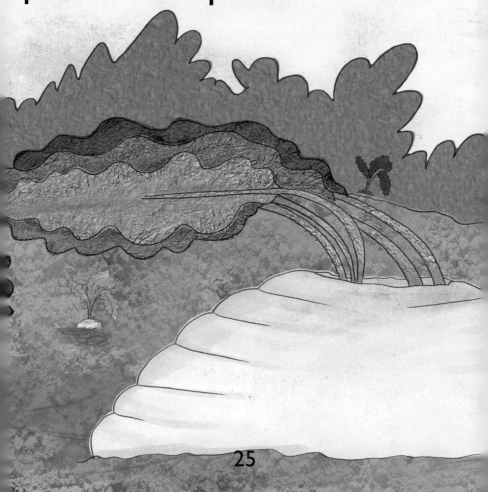

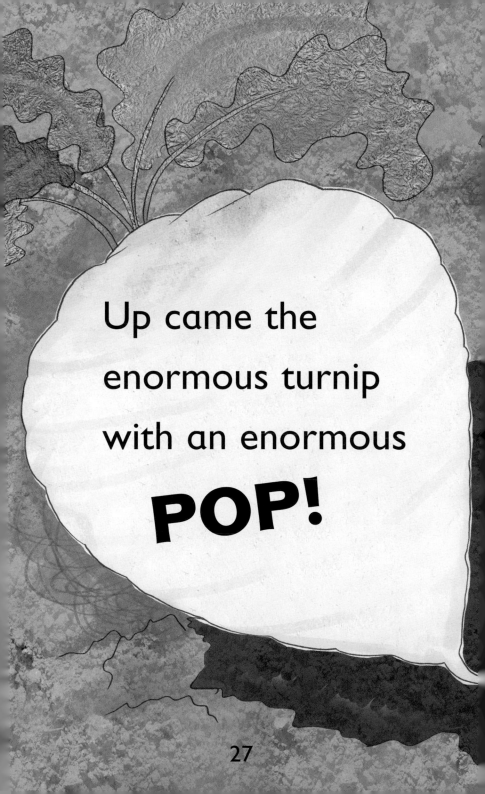

Up came the
enormous turnip
with an enormous
POP!

Then they all had turnip
soup for supper ...

and breakfast,

and
lunch,

and tea!

Puzzle 1

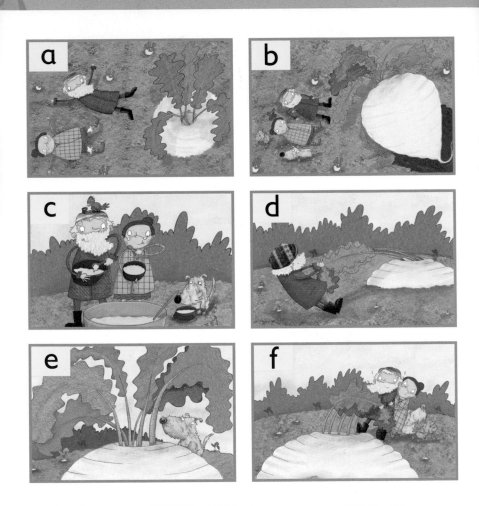

Put these pictures in the correct order.
Now tell the story in your own words.
What different endings can you think of?

Puzzle 2

young old
hardworking

lazy strong
helpful

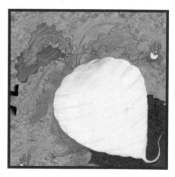

tiny huge
minute

Choose the correct adjectives for each character or object. Which adjectives are incorrect? Turn over to find the answers.

Answers

Puzzle 1

The correct order is: 1d, 2e, 3a, 4c, 5f, 6b

Puzzle 2

Chicken Licken: the correct adjective is foolish

The incorrect adjectives are calm, clever

Foxy Loxy: the correct adjectives are cunning, sly

The incorrect adjective is generous

Ducky Lucky: the correct adjective is silly

The incorrect adjectives are careful, wise

Look out for Leapfrog fairy tales:

Cinderella
ISBN 978 0 7496 4228 0

The Three Little Pigs
ISBN 978 0 7496 4227 3

Jack and the Beanstalk
ISBN 978 0 7496 4229 7

The Three Billy Goats Gruff
ISBN 978 0 7496 4226 6

Goldilocks and the Three Bears
ISBN 978 0 7496 4225 9

Little Red Riding Hood
ISBN 978 0 7496 4224 2

Rapunzel
ISBN 978 0 7496 6159 5

Snow White
ISBN 978 0 7496 6161 8

The Emperor's New Clothes
ISBN 978 0 7496 6163 2

The Pied Piper of Hamelin
ISBN 978 0 7496 6164 9

Hansel and Gretel
ISBN 978 0 7496 6162 5

The Sleeping Beauty
ISBN 978 0 7496 6160 1

Rumpelstiltskin
ISBN 978 0 7496 6165 6

The Ugly Duckling
ISBN 978 0 7496 6166 3

Puss in Boots
ISBN 978 0 7496 6167 0

The Frog Prince
ISBN 978 0 7496 6168 7

The Princess and the Pea
ISBN 978 0 7496 6169 4

Dick Whittington
ISBN 978 0 7496 6170 0

The Little Match Girl
ISBN 978 0 7496 6582 1

The Elves and the Shoemaker
ISBN 978 0 7496 6581 4

The Little Mermaid
ISBN 978 0 7496 6583 8

The Little Red Hen
ISBN 978 0 7496 6585 2

The Nightingale
ISBN 978 0 7496 6586 9

Thumbelina
ISBN 978 0 7496 6587 6

The Magic Porridge Pot
ISBN 978 0 7496 8611 6

The Enormous Turnip
ISBN 978 0 7496 8612 3

Chicken Licken
ISBN 978 0 7496 8613 0

The Three Wishes
ISBN 978 0 7496 8614 7

The Big Pancake
ISBN 978 0 7496 8615 4

The Gingerbread Man
ISBN 978 0 7496 8616 1